BIG BROTHER, LITTLE BROTHER

Story and pictures by **MARCI CURTIS**

DIAL BOOKS FOR YOUNG READERS ✦ **NEW YORK**

For Rodney—best hubby, best friend, best soul mate 'til the end.

Big thanks to the big and little brothers:

Sam and **N**ate, **A**lejandro and **A**ntonio, **J**esse and **M**iles, **Z**ack and **A**li, and my nephews **C**aleb and **A**sher—
it was a pleasure watching you all grow up!

And thanks, too, to the parents and siblings of these wonderful boys and to the big and little sisters hiding in the book.

Published by Dial Books for Young Readers • A division of Penguin Young Readers Group
345 Hudson Street • New York, New York 10014
Copyright © 2004 by Marci Curtis • All rights reserved • Text set in Triplex
Manufactured in China on acid-free paper
Library of Congress Cataloging-in-Publication Data • Curtis, Marci.
Big brother, little brother / story and pictures by Marci Curtis. • p.   cm.
Summary: Photographs and rhyming text show both the fun and trials of having a big or little brother.
ISBN 0-8037-2870-0 • [1. Brothers—Fiction. 2. Stories in rhyme.] I. Title. PZ8.3.C93445Bg 2004 [E]—dc21   2003009102
1 3 5 7 9 10 8 6 4 2

Big brother, little brother, buddies true and strong.
Life is truly twice as fun since he came along.

Little brother, open wide! WORMS **taste just like chicken.**

Aim your foot, add some power — now you're really KiCkin'!

Big brother blowing bubbles **while we do the dishes.**

Get off, little brother, before our pumpkin *squishes*.

Big brother creams me in a pillow fight.

Make two loops, yank 'em tight! Yup, that knot looks right.

Big brother is my topsy-turvy buddy.

I'm going to get you nice and *muddy.

Little brother's got huge MUSCLES **just like me!**

Kiss my *fish*, make a wish, then I'll set him free.

Big brother and I race home *neck* and *neck*.

Watch Out!, brother! You'll get more than a peck!

Little brother's working hard to fix my SUPER powers.

Let's bring Mom the pretty part of her favorite flowers.

Little brother, don't you **DARE**! Hands off my underwear!

We're munching hanging **donuts** dangling in the air.

Big brother sits with me my first time on the **.**

Tug his **tail** little brother—and maybe he'll pull us?

Little brother drools, but I've got super-spit.

Ready now, steady now—get that hit !

Big brother's there for me when I start to cry.

Go ahead. Don't be scared. It's just a butterfly.

Big brother has the fastest peel in the West.

Which brother's belly **BULGES** out the best?

Big brother and I, adopted from the **start**.

Though we're not blood brothers, we are brothers of the heart.

Little brother looks like me, but we are NOT the same.

I have **5** and you have **1**—isn't *that* a shame?

Big brother, little brother, our adventures never end.
We'll always have each other and you'll always be my friend.